The Halloween Cat

by Christine Ricci
illustrated by Zina Saunders

Ready-to-Read

Simon Spotlight/Nick Jr.

New York   London   Toronto   Sydney

Based on the TV series *Dora the Explorer*® as seen on Nick Jr.®

SIMON SPOTLIGHT
An imprint of Simon & Schuster Children's Publishing Division
1230 Avenue of the Americas
New York, New York 10020
Copyright © 2004 Viacom International Inc. All rights reserved.
NICKELODEON, NICK JR., *Dora the Explorer,* and all related titles, logos, and characters
are registered trademarks of Viacom International Inc.
All rights reserved, including the right of reproduction in whole or in part in any form.
READY-TO-READ, SIMON SPOTLIGHT, and colophon are
registered trademarks of Simon & Schuster, Inc.
Manufactured in the United States of America
6 8 10 9 7 5

Library of Congress Cataloging-in-Publication Data
Ricci, Christine.
The Halloween cat / by Christine Ricci ; [illustrated by] Zina Saunders.—1st ed.
p. cm. —(Ready-to-read)
"Based on the TV series Dora the Explorer as seen on Nick Jr"—T.p. verso.
Summary: Dora and Boots help a small black cat find its way home to the Candy Castle on
Halloween. Features rebuses.
ISBN 0-689-86799-9 (pbk.)
1. Rebuses. [1. Halloween—Fiction. 2. Cats—Fiction. 3. Rebuses.] I. Saunders, Zina, ill.
II. Dora the explorer (Television program) III. Title. IV. Ready-to-read. Level 1,
Dora the explorer.
PZ7.R355 Hal 2004
[E]—dc22
2003018335

Hi, I am .

DORA

I am dressed as a

DINOSAUR

for Halloween.

 is dressed as a !

BOOTS   BANANA

We see a small 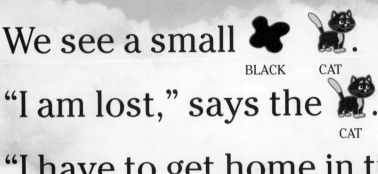.

BLACK   CAT

"I am lost," says the 🐱.

CAT

"I have to get home in time for the big Halloween party!"

and I will help the 🐱.

BOOTS

CAT

Will you help too?

The  knows where
the 🐱 lives.
MAP

CAT

"The 🐱 lives in the
CAT

🏰 with the 🧙 ,"
CANDY CASTLE   GOOD WITCH

says 📜 .
MAP

We have to go to the
HAUNTED HOUSE
and into the to get to
SPOOKY FOREST
the .
CANDY CASTLE

We are at the  .

HAUNTED HOUSE

It is dark inside!

We need something to

help us see in the dark.

Can you spot the ?

FLASHLIGHT

There are many DOORS

in the HAUNTED HOUSE .

A says, "Find the

GHOST   DOOR

with 7 ."

SEVEN   SPIDERS

Yay! We made it out of the  .

HAUNTED HOUSE

Now we will go to the  .

SPOOKY FOREST

Do you see the ?

SPOOKY FOREST

Uh-oh, here is a .

GATE

 says an

MAP   ORANGE   KEY

will open the .

GATE

Do you see an  ORANGE KEY?

Watch out!

SWIPER will try to swipe the KEY.

Say " SWIPER, no swiping!"

Yay! We stopped 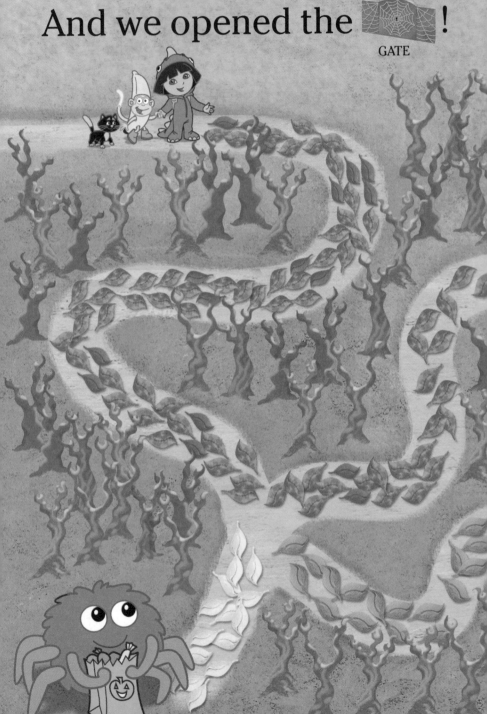.
And we opened the !

SWIPER

GATE

 says the

MAP   RED   LEAVES

will lead us out of the

 .

SPOOKY FOREST

We made it out of the ⟨SPOOKY FOREST⟩ !

Now we have to find .

CANDY CASTLE

Here we are at  .

CANDY CASTLE

But how do we get in?

"Use the  !" says

BROOMSTICK

the  .

CAT

Wow! We are flying!

Hello,  !

GOOD WITCH

We did it! The  CAT is home
with the GOOD WITCH.
Happy Halloween!